Contents

Early Days

Early Days

· ·

This is the tale of John, whose mother loved
him very much. And that was just as well
because no one else thought much of him.
It wasn't that he did anything wrong. He
didn't do anything at all – except eat four
times a day and sleep in between.

Every morning he would open his big blue
eyes to see what was for breakfast, and when
that was done, he closed them again and
nodded off until lunch.

"Your baby's so quiet," the neighbours
said. And John's mother nodded. He was
very quiet. He drowsed in the dark and he
snoozed in the sun; he kipped in the kitchen
and yawned in the yard; his forty winks lasted
from dawn to dusk; he hibernated in the
winter and in the summer too. From his head
to his toes he was comatose and when he was

static, he was ecstatic. He was calm, he was tranquil – he was tranquillized! The bed, the bench, the old rocking-chair – it was all the same to him, but his favourite dossing-place was the old rag rug by the fireplace, where he lay and breathed in and out so steadily his mother never had to use the bellows on the fire. He could keep the blaze going all day, as long as his mother put coal on now and then.

This was how she found out her son could talk. One day when she was pegging out the clothes she heard him call, "Mother! Mother!"

"What is it, John, lad?" she shouted as she came in through the washhouse.

"Can you turn me round, please? I'm burning all down one side."

What with sleeping and eating, John grew and grew. When he was five he stretched from end to end and side to side of the old rag rug.

"Why, he's a great useless lump," said the neighbours. "He'll never come to anything."

"Well, he'll come to no harm, then," replied his mother.

She looked down at her son and said fondly, "Our John's going to be special. You wait and see."

"We'll have to," answered the neighbours. "He'll come to nothing if it don't come to him. He'll be late for his own funeral. Bone idle, that's his trouble."

And after that, being familiar, everyone called him

IDLE JACK.

Jack – Star Pupil

Jack – Star Pupil

One Sunday, when Idle Jack was about ten years old, six foot tall, a yard wide and just as much of a slowcoach as ever, his mother said, "John, lad, tomorrow you must start school and learn all there is to learn. Then you can go out in the wide world and earn your living."

Jack stopped breathing on the fire and making it glow cherry red, and looked up with his bright blue eyes.

"Why, Mother?" he asked.

"Because otherwise you're going to eat me out of house and home."

So Jack, who would do anything to please his mother except stay awake, agreed.

"Now you listen to me, our John," his mother went on. "Remember these three things and you can't go wrong. Keep your eyes open, smile nicely and never disagree with anybody."

Jack nodded. At least, his mother thought he was nodding: really he was nodding off.

But next day, at nine o'clock sharp, Jack rolled into school. His mother took him to the top of the hill at five to, and rolled him down, just to make sure.

Every boy and girl in the class cheered and laughed when Jack arrived and the teacher said, "So, you're Jack, are you?"

Jack opened his eyes, smiled nicely at the teacher and said, "That's right, Ma'am."

At first, knowing what boys are like, always up to some villainy or other, Teacher put Jack at the front of the class.

But that didn't work very well. Not because of Jack, who was as good as gold. No, it was the others. The bad lads all shifted their places to sit behind him, playing jacks and chewing gum and making rude drawings. And our Jack was so broad Teacher couldn't see what they were up to. (As it happened they were a bit too smart and gave the game away by sniggering at their own jokes.)

So Teacher moved Jack to the back of the class where no one could hide behind him. And it used to cheer her up no end to see him sitting there, beaming like the sun in the sky. He did seem a bit slow and didn't learn very much, but there was good reason for that. Most of the time he was fast asleep, inside, and Teacher was quite unaware of this because he was looking at her and smiling so blissfully.

Teachers think the world of pupils who are good-tempered and don't misbehave. Mostly, then, Teacher left him alone and kept her eye on the bad lads. But every now and then, so he wouldn't feel neglected, she'd ask Jack a question.

This could have spelt trouble for him, but one of the girls, who had a soft spot for Jack, would give him a kick, just a little tap, on the ankle. Then Jack would wake up inside and say very politely, "That's right, Ma'am," or

"Whatever you say, Ma'am."

So, while she reckoned Jack was perhaps a little slow on the uptake, Teacher gave him a gold star for conduct. She wasn't to know that he was asleep most of the time. But what you don't know can't upset you, can it?

So Jack was star pupil and the boys and girls liked him. After all, he was twice as big as any of them, though he wouldn't harm a fly.

But there's always an exception to every rule, and the exception was a lad called Sam, big and disagreeable, a real bully. Sam could not abide Jack. The more popular Jack became, the more he hated him.

So one day, being cunning, he hit on the idea of making a fool of him.

"You're star pupil, right?" he said.

"That's right, Sam," answered Jack.

"Then you can race me round Hundred Acre Wood, can't you?" said Sam, winking at the others who were standing round.

"Anything you say."

Sam looked at the rest and tapped the side of his head. The others all laughed, for they knew Sam could run like the wind.

"I'll give you fifty yards' start, Jack."

"That's right, Sam."

So, after school, off they all went to Hundred Acre Wood. Sam and Jack put their coats down to mark the start – which was also the finish – which saved a lot of trouble and coats.

"Ten times round and the loser has to kiss the winner's boots, right?" said Sam, winking at the others. Some felt sorry for Jack, but they all laughed.

Jack answered, "Right you are, Sam," and ambled off.

As soon as Jack had gone round the bend in the trees, Sam set off at a gallop with the crowd cheering.

Sam went scorching round the edge of the wood, expecting to see Jack puffing along in front. But there was no sign of him. Sam put on speed, round the next turning and the next. As he came in sight of the crowd by the markers, he shouted, "Where's he gone to?" and they answered, "He's up ahead there, Sam. After him! You'll soon catch up."

Sure enough, there was Jack just disappearing round the bend.

Sam leapt off in pursuit like a hound, with the crowd cheering him on. But as he turned the corner, there was no Jack in sight.

Sam put on speed. By now he was snorting like a bull, but he kept going full tilt right to the end of the lap. And the crowd shouted, "Just ahead, Sam. You're gaining on him, hand over fist. Go for it, boy!"

Round and round the track went Sam, three, four, five, six times, till all the puff was gone from him and he was almost on his knees. But he never overtook Jack.

For Jack hadn't gone more than twenty yards before he began to yawn and his knees began to buckle. He wandered off the track, rolled down a bank and fell asleep under a bush. Every now and then the other lads' yelling roused him, so up he got, staggered through the trees and out the other side of the wood and carried on round the course, wondering all the time when Sam was going to pass him.

At long last, when the sun was going down, he tripped over something in the grass. It was Sam, lying there, completely worn out. Jack felt so sorry for him that, sleepy as he was, he picked Sam up, slung him over his shoulders and walked round to the finishing line.

"Good old Jack," they shouted.

Poor old Sam, he didn't even have the puff left to kiss Jack's boots. It was an awful humiliation. For now Jack was star pupil and champion athlete as well. But that wasn't the end of the story.

Next day, in the school yard, Sam, looking very aggravated, said to Jack, "So you're star pupil, eh?"

"That's right, Sam."

"And you're champion runner, eh?"

"Anything you say, Sam."

"Right, well, I'm going to knock your block off, see?"

"Fair enough, Sam," said Jack.

Everyone trooped round to the wall where Teacher couldn't see, and Sam didn't wait for them to drop the handkerchief but started in, hitting Jack like a punch bag, kicking as well. Jack just let him bang away, because standing up against the wall made him feel sleepy. His eyelids went down but he kept a nice smile on his face.

This only made Sam more furious. He pulled back about three yards and charged at Jack like a bull, head down, aiming for his nose. But just as he got there, Jack fell right asleep and slid down the wall. Sam's head hit the brickwork full tilt and he was out like a light.

Jack carried him back into the classroom. The teacher looked at the big bump on Sam's head and asked, "Did you do that, Jack?"

"That's right, Ma'am," Jack answered.

"You're a wicked boy, Jack."

"Whatever you say, Ma'am."

"Don't you answer back, my lad," snapped the teacher. She'd begun to suspect that Jack was making a monkey out of her. And teachers don't like that.

"You're the wickedest boy in the school. Any more trouble from you and I shall send you home."

There wasn't any more trouble. As long as Jack was at school he stayed star pupil, champion athlete, best fighter and the wickedest boy. You can't go further up the tree than that. And most of the time he was asleep anyway.

The only person who wasn't on Jack's side was Sam, and he couldn't do anything about it. He was as sick as a parrot.

And the neighbours. They were as sour as cream left in the sun. They told Jack's mum, "You wait. He'll come to a bad end." But she only said, "No, not our John."

Jack Earns a Living

Jack Earns a Living

Now the day came at last when Jack's mother said to him, "Our John, there's nothing for it, lad. You'll have to go and earn a living, or you'll eat me out of house and home."

"Right you are, Mother," answered Jack, cheerfully. After all, he was fourteen years old now and big as a barn door. And in those days, you earned your bread at fourteen, not like nowadays when they all loaf around at school, cheeking the teachers.

The trouble was, where should he go? Round the village he already had a name and it wasn't for hard work.

So his mother sent him to a farm outside Little Piddock where they'd never heard of Jack. And before he left home she told him, "Now listen, our John. Whatever the master gives you tonight, even if it's only a penny, wrap it up in your hankie and stick it in your pocket. That way you won't lose it."

Off he went, but what with forty winks here and there it was nearly midday before he arrived.

The farmer set him to mucking out the barn while the cattle were in the meadow. He set to with a will, but soon all the exertion – shovelling what the cows had left behind – tired him out and he fell fast asleep. He only woke up when Bluebell led the other ladies into the stalls and gave him a good lick on the nose.

You can imagine the master wasn't too pleased. But Jack had done a bit of work before he dropped off, so he told him, "Look, Jack lad, I can't pay you, but here's a jar of buttermilk to take home to your mother."

Now Jack, like a good boy, remembered what his mother had said that morning and he did what he was told. He spread out his red and white spotted handkerchief and poured the buttermilk into it. Then he knotted the hankie and pushed it into his pocket, holding the jar in his hand.

As he marched along, he could feel the buttermilk running down inside his trousers. But he was more worried about disobeying his mother than getting wet legs.

When he arrived back home and his mother saw what had happened, she shook her head.

"Oh, John, lad, why didn't you carry it home on your head?"

"Never mind, Mother, I'll do that next time," answered Jack.

Next day, she roused him at dawn and sent him off to another farm, on the other side of the village.

Once again, he was a little bit late (round about three hours). His new master took one look at him and sent him to feed the pigs. Later on that day he found Jack sound asleep with his head against the flanks of the old black sow.

"You'd better get off home, my lad," said

the farmer, " 'cause you're no use to me here."

"But what about my wages, master?" asked Jack.

The farmer looked at him and Jack looked back with his round blue eyes.

"I'm not daft enough to pay you for today, Jack, but here's something to take home for your mother."

The farmer gave Jack an old cat, too idle to catch mice any more but still with a bit of spirit in her. Jack wasn't going to be caught out this time. He put the old cat on top of his thatch, just as his mother had told him, and set off home.

Well, the old cat didn't fancy that at all. She slid off Jack's head, scratched his nose in three places and shot down the lane, back to the farm they'd just come from.

When Jack's mother heard what had happened, she said, "John, lad, why ever didn't you tie it on a string and lead it behind you?"

"Right you are, Mother. I'll remember next

time," said Jack, cheerful as ever.

And he did. Next day was more or less like the others, except that what the farmer gave him to take home was a shoulder of mutton. The lad tied it with string, just as his mother had said, and led it along behind him.

All went well until he was in sight of home, when all the village dogs lined up behind him to have first bite at his wages. All that was left when he came in through the back door of the cottage was the bone.

Jack's mother was speechless – well, almost.

"Oh, our John, why didn't you carry it home safe on your shoulder?"

"Right you are, Mother," he answered. "That's what I'll do tomorrow."

Poor Widow Patch didn't know where to turn. The neighbours were smirking behind their hands. Jack was turning out just as they'd said.

Next day was Friday and she decided to give Jack one last chance before she gave up on him. When she woke him up at dawn, she told him, "Off you go, our John. Do your best."

And so he did – his very best. He was only two hours late for work. The farmer sent him out in the meadow to turn the hay so it would dry in the sun. And Jack kept going until noon when the heat of the sun and the soft inviting heaps of hay got the better of him and down he went.

Now the master couldn't say he hadn't tried. But he wouldn't pay him money. So he thought a bit and then he remembered a little old donkey he had tied up in the barnyard, too small for carrying loads and too bad-tempered to put in a cart.

He gave it to Jack, and Jack, without a word, took the donkey by its forelegs and its hindlegs and swung it up on his shoulders.

All went well, and he was just getting into the village, when who should he meet but Sam and some of the other lads who'd been at school with him. Sam's mouth fell open.

Then he burst out laughing.

"Will you look at that gormless idiot?" he crowed.

And they all looked and they all laughed until they fell about and rolled over the road. Then one of them, who was a bit kinder than the others, called, "You idiot! You ride the donkey, you don't carry him!"

So Jack put the donkey down and got on its back. Well, the donkey was so small and he was so large that his feet touched the ground. But they got along somehow or other until they came past the school cottage. And there, sitting in the porch, was the teacher. She nearly fell off her rocking-chair.

"Jack," she said. "I always thought you were a wicked boy – now I know for sure. Get down off that poor little beast before you crush it to death."

Now Jack always did what he was told, so he stood up straight and the donkey ran out from between his legs, giving Jack a nice nip on his rear portions before kicking up its heels and galloping away down the road.

So, Jack went home without his pay.

Jack's mother said nothing because, to tell the truth, she was stuck for words. She had a good think about it all over the weekend, then on Monday morning she told Jack he'd have to go right away to work.

And she meant right away. She had a cousin, a distant cousin, one who lived twenty miles off, on the road towards the big city. She sent word to him and back came the answer that her boy would be welcome to come and stay – in fact he had just the job for Jack.

Jack was overjoyed at this and he made ready for the journey. His mother packed him up his nightshirt and an extra pair of socks and gave him a red jumper which she'd knitted. On it she'd stitched in blue letters: *My name is John Patch and I live at Hill Cottage, Little Piddock*, in case he forgot. Jack promised to send home to his mother half of what he earned and off he ambled.

★   ★   ★

His new master looked him up and down, with his broad shoulders and his big smile, and asked him, "Well, John, what can you do?"

Jack scratched his head and smiled.

"Whatever you say, master."

"Well, can you keep still and keep your eyes open?"

Jack's head started to nod, so the farmer said, "Well, you can be my night-watchman, then. Sit outside the hen-house at night. Keep your eyes open, watch the door like a hawk, for the old fox is about."

"Right you are, master," said Jack and that night he sat outside the hen-house, fast asleep. He didn't let that door out of his sight, and round about four in the morning the old fox turned up, saw this great lump of a lad sitting there with his eyes open, didn't like it and went away again.

Next day, the farmer was pleased as punch.

"You're a good lad, our John."

The next night was the same, and the next. As the summer went by the farmer got more and more pleased with Jack and even wrote to his mother to say so. She showed the letter to her neighbours and they were so green with envy they could have spat. All they could say was, "You wait."

Summer went, autumn came. The farmer was happy. The fox wasn't. And to tell the truth, neither was Jack. It was getting chilly outside at nights, in fact it was so cold, Jack wasn't even sleeping.

Till one night he had a bright idea.

"Farmer said, 'watch the door', right?" he asked himself. And he got a very sensible answer. He took the door off its hinges and carted it into the barn where the wind and the rain couldn't get and there was plenty of warm hay to lie on. Our Jack slept like a log, with the door propped up in front of him and his eyes fixed on it.

In the morning the farmer found the old fox had paid a call. The hen-house was full of feathers and not much else.

His first thought was to give Jack a good thrashing. But his second thought was not to, because Jack was nearly twice as big as he was, so he said, "It won't do, John. You're a dead loss as a night-watchman and you're useless for ought else. You'll have to go."

"Right you are, master," said Jack. "But what about my pay? I'd like some money, if you please – not milk, nor cheese, nor a cat, nor a leg of mutton, nor a nasty old donkey."

The farmer looked at him and decided it was best not to argue. So he said, "Here's five guineas for you to send home to your mother. Only promise me one thing."

"What's that, master?" asked Jack, eager to please.

"Don't tell anyone else I paid you. They'll all say I've gone mad, which I probably have. So here you are." He handed Jack five gold coins. "Keep it under your hat – not a word."

So Jack put his five guineas under his hat, said goodbye and set off down the road.

Jack's Funeral

Jack's Funeral

· ·

Jack said to himself, "If I can earn five guineas, why not ten? That's five for Mother and five for me."

So instead of going home, he tramped on down the road towards the city. The bigger the town, he thought, the more doors to look after.

But, just as he came near the city, he saw a marvellous sight. Trotting down the highway were six white horses, pulling a big blue open carriage. Seated in it were a splendid couple – a big man with a gold crown, white hair and a red face, and a lovely girl with red hair bound in a silver circlet and flashing green eyes.

Jack gawped and goggled and thought to himself, Oh, I do like the look of her.

And quite right too. For this was the king himself and his daughter, Esmerelda, and as the coach clattered past, the princess looked down at the big lad by the wayside. It seemed to Jack that she gave him a special smile. His insides turned to jelly.

Without a second's thought, he whipped off his hat and bowed deeply. And, as his head went down, his five guineas slid off into the dust on the road.

With his head bent, Jack didn't see who had just come along the highway – a fierce-looking soldier in a red coat with a sword and pistol in his belt.

Jack bent down to pick up his rolling coins just the moment before the soldier bent down, with the very same aim. For here was a man who didn't mind how he picked up a living.

Money safely back in his fist, Jack straightened up. His big head, rising through the air, met the trooper's chin coming down. Jack's noddle rang like a peal of bells, but he stayed upright, while the other chap went base over apex on the road.

"I do beg your pardon," said Jack, helping him up again.

"You blank-blank-blank fool," swore the soldier. He was most put out. It was bad enough not getting his paws on the gold, without getting clouted into the bargain. "D'you think I'm invisible or something?"

Remembering what his mother had told him, Jack smiled and said, "Right you are, friend."

"What d'you mean, right you are? D'you take me for an idiot, you pig basher?"

"Anything you say, your honour," answered Jack.

"Would you like a thick ear?" demanded the trooper.

"Just as you please," Jack told him. And the next thing he knew he was lying flat on his back, with another seven bells ringing in his head. The soldier had given him a great wallop with his pistol butt and was just following that with a couple of smart kicks when someone close by roared, "Soldier!"

He sprang to attention, quickly stowing his pistol in his belt. Jack, still muzzy, looked up. There stood the gentleman from the carriage. And what a splendid figure he was – every inch a king, every foot a ruler. But Jack's eyes were only on the princess, who stood a little way off.

"You've killed him, soldier," bellowed the king.

"No, sire, honestly, he's just unconscious." The soldier was very humble now.

"No, he's not. His eyes are open."

"Yes, sire, but look, he's smiling."

"None of your lip, soldier." The king did not like being contradicted.

"Father," said the princess, stepping forward. "We can soon see if the poor lad's dead," and she took out a mirror and held it close to Jack's open mouth to check whether his breathing would cloud the glass. Well, of course, the sight of that gorgeous face so near his own took Jack's breath away.

"The poor boy's gone," said the princess,

holding up the mirror. At these words, the soldier fell on his knees.

"Spare me, sire. It was an accident and he hit me first."

The king thought a moment. "Very well. But you must pay the lad's mother one hundred guineas."

"His address is on his jumper," added Princess Esmerelda, who was a helpful girl.

"But first," growled the king, "go and get the undertaker to make the lad a nice coffin. Come, my dear."

And with that they climbed back into the carriage and rode away.

The soldier, muttering to himself, slouched off to the town and ordered the coffin. It cost him five guineas, which hurt him very much.

Right, thought he, that comes out of the hundred for a start.

Then he thought a bit more. *Nobody'll know if I only give that fool's mother fifty guineas.*

And with that notion in his head he

went off to the tavern and had a drink. And another. And every drink he took, he knocked ten guineas off what he thought Jack's mother ought to get. By the evening, the old lady was almost out of pocket!

While the soldier was drinking, the undertaker's men took the coffin down to the high road. There they found Jack as large as life (or as death, as the case may be). With a bit of a shove and a push, they got him fixed inside, then found they'd forgotten the lid. So off they went back to town and left Jack lying there.

Well, after an hour or so he heard a voice, and there standing by the coffin was an apprentice.

"What're you doing there, stupid?" the apprentice demanded in a charming way.

Jack smiled at him. "Why, I'm earning my mother a hundred guineas."

"What?" The lad's greedy eyes glittered. "Just by lying there?"

"That's it. Simple as you like. Better than

watching doors," said Jack.

The apprentice gave him a funny look, then said, "How about swapping with me? I'll give you ten shillings."

"Just as you like," answered Jack and struggled out of the box. The other gave him the money, and settled down in his place, thinking, This is the life, a hundred guineas for ten shillings. These pig bashers didn't understand money like city folk. And while he was thinking this great thought he dozed off.

Jack wandered off towards the town and just after he'd gone, back came the two undertaker's men. They stopped by the coffin and looked down at the apprentice lying there.

"He looks different," said one. "He's shrunk."

"That's rigor mortis, boy," said the other, who'd been in the trade longer. "Help us put this lid on."

So they lidded the box, then lifted it up.

It was lighter than they expected and so they got a move on, heading towards the graveyard, because it was getting near evening now.

On their way they passed Jack, who was lying asleep in the grass.

"He looks like that bloke in here used to look," said one of the men. "Happen we've made a mistake."

But the other, the one with more experience, answered, "We've been paid to bury one bloke, not two."

Their talking woke Jack and being curious, he got up and followed them, a little way behind, to the graveyard.

By the time they'd put the coffin down they were fagged out. The older one said, "How about a drink before we dig the hole, eh?"

So, off they went to the tavern. And who should they meet there but the soldier, busy robbing Jack's mother (in his mind, that is). By this time, he'd had a drop or two, so he got them to sit down with him. He felt like celebrating for he'd saved himself the best part of one hundred guineas that afternoon.

One drink led to another. Then they started playing cards and gambling. By sunset, they were hard at it and the table was covered with bottles and cards and gold pieces.

Meanwhile, Jack wandered into the graveyard. It's not everyone who has the chance of going to his own funeral, so he was curious. But as he got closer to the coffin he heard a noise. Someone was knocking, banging and shouting. Yet he couldn't see a door anywhere. And if there was ever a lad with an eye for doors, it was our Jack.

Then he had to laugh, for it occurred to him that all the noise was coming from the coffin. The bloke inside wanted to get out. So Jack, being an amiable sort of lad, prised up the lid and set him free.

At first the apprentice was angry and wanted his money back, but when he looked

at Jack and saw how big he was, he changed
his mind and said, instead, "I reckon you owe
me a drink, boy."

"Right you are," said Jack, and off they
went to the tavern. By that time the place was
lit up and so were the soldier and the two
undertaker's men.

When the door opened and first Jack, then
the apprentice, came in, the soldier jumped
up and swore.

"Blank me, that's the bloke I topped. He's
come for me."

And without waiting another second, he
barged out into the night.

The undertaker's men were a bit slower on
the uptake. But they jumped up too and said,
"That's the bloke we put in the coffin."

Without waiting another second, they
barged out too, leaving the table, the money,
the cards and the bottles.

So Jack and the apprentice took over the
game where the others had left off and at
the end of the day they split twenty guineas

between them. When they left the tavern, the apprentice nudged Jack and said, "You're a lad and a half, ain't you?"

"If you say so," answered Jack.

Two days later, Jack's mother was sitting outside her cottage talking to her neighbours – about Jack, of course.

"I don't reckon you'll see much of that good-for-nothing son of yours," said one. "He's not sent you a penny back, has he?"

"Oh, our John's all right," said his mother. Then she looked up the road. "Well now, what's that soldier coming up here for?"

Sure enough, up marched the soldier and saluted.

"Are you the widow Patch?" he said. She nodded. "Well," he began, then he stopped. He couldn't say, "I'm afraid your son's dead, ma'am," because he'd seen him. So he said, "I've come on your son's behalf. Er – he sent you this."

The neighbours stared a bit. But when the

soldier put down a big bag which clinked and chinked, their eyes nearly popped out of their heads.

"What did I tell you?" said Jack's mother.

Jack and the Lion

Jack and the Lion

· ·

Now Jack, as you know, had never been in
the big city before. So he wandered round the
streets for a few days, eating a hearty meal
now and then, and looking out the best spots
for a quiet kip.

After a while, though, he began to wonder
what he ought to do next. What he didn't
know was that this was being sorted out for
him, right there and then.

All unbeknown to Jack, in the throne room
of the palace in the main square of the town,
the king and Esmerelda were having a bit of
an argument. It began when the king told his
daughter, "Time for you to get married, my
dear."

"Why, Father?" she asked him. "I'm quite
content as I am."

"Oh, pooh," he said. "What's that got to do

with it? You've got to get married."

"But why?"

"Well, who'd rule the country if I fell off the twig, eh? Tell me that."

"Why, I would," said Esmerelda.

The king stared, then he laughed so much he choked on his breakfast bacon.

"No, no, no, my love. Married you shall be – we have to have a king. It says so in the books."

Esmerelda rolled her eyes to the ceiling.

"If you say so, Father. But who's it going to be?"

"Why, we set a test and the one who passes it gets you and half the kingdom."

"What sort of test?"

This foxed the king for a moment, then he remembered.

"Why, the man who rescues you from a wicked enchanter wins the honour."

"But I'm not captured by a wicked enchanter. There hasn't been one round here for years."

The king had to admit she was right. Then he brightened up.

"The man who can cure you from a mysterious illness."

"But I haven't had a day's illness in my life, barring measles and chicken pox."

"No more you haven't, girl."

There was a pause for thought, then the king said, "The man who can make you laugh."

But Esmerelda crowed and said, "Father, I'm always laughing. Almost any man makes me laugh."

That was true enough. The king was properly banjaxed.

"All right, my love. What do you suggest? It's got to be something that sorts out the sheep from the goats."

"Father," said Esmerelda, "I'm meant to be wedding, not starting a farm."

The king decided he'd had enough of the argument. "Tomorrow," he said, "we'll make a proclamation."

★   ★   ★

Next day the proclamation was posted round the city. It said that the king's fair daughter, Esmerelda, would give her hand (and the rest of her) in marriage to the first suitor who would perform a feat of heroism beyond human endurance.

The proclamation didn't say what sort of feat, because the king hadn't worked that out, but it was enough to make most of the eligible bachelors in the city think twice and decide not to apply.

So, on the following day, when the suitors turned up in the throne room where the king and Princess Esmerelda were sitting, there were only three of them.

One was a duke, very military-looking with a red face. The second was a professor, with a long nose. And the third was a lad in a red jumper with his name and address stitched on it.

The king looked them over. He knew the first two, but didn't recognize the third, partly because he had a short memory (most kings do) and partly because when he'd last seen this lad he was lying down and now he was standing up. But Esmerelda recognized the third suitor right away, and though she was a touch surprised, she said nothing. She gave him a big smile and got one back.

"Very good," said the king. "Now listen. The one who performs this feat of heroism beyond human endurance wins the hand of the fair Esmerelda. Is that clear?"

There was a moment's silence, then the duke stepped forward. "Agreed, sire, but may one ask what is this feat? I'll set off right away and perform it."

"Ha, hm," said the king. "One doesn't just think up such a feat off the top of one's head, you know."

"But..." began the duke. However, he got no further because the professor interrupted him.

"Majesty, right at this moment, roaming in the forest is a savage lion, escaped from a circus. Because of his treatment, this lion has become so hostile to human beings that he cannot even set eyes on one without tearing him limb from limb."

At this the duke turned pale and was about to object, when the professor nudged him and said to the king, "Tonight, all three of your daughter's ardent suitors will venture into the forest. Tomorrow, one of us will emerge, bearing the lion's mortal remains."

At this, Esmerelda turned pale. But the king said, "Splendid. That'll be the one. Off you go, then!"

The three suitors bowed and left the throne room.

Once outside, the duke turned to the professor and demanded, "Are you mad? This is certain death."

The professor looked at the duke with the utmost contempt, then answered, very quietly, "Leave it to me – this lion will solve all our problems."

Then, raising his voice, he said to Jack,

"My good fellow. Meet us at the city gate at sunset."

"Right you are," answered Jack.

...hree suitors set off
...fessor led the way,
...uke, with Jack (who
...ling along behind.
...spered the professor
...is clodhopper go
...n's eating him, we
...ck and drag it to the

...e, then about five
...mind had caught up,
...aves two of us. How

...is head at such
...w lots, you and I.
...points the other
...asury. That way, we divide
the riches of the kingdom between us."

The duke didn't quite follow this cunning

God Knows My Name!

You have searched me, LORD, and you know me. Psalm 139v1

plot, but he couldn't think of anything better, so he kept quiet. By now, all three of them were getting near the lion's den, so they were all on the quiet side anyway.

On the edge of a big clearing with a pool in the middle, the two plotters waited for Jack to catch up with them. Then the professor said, "You're youngest, my boy. You get first go. You hide here and wait till dawn. When the lion comes to drink at the pool, you capture him. We'll wait close at hand, in case you need help."

"Right you are, sir," said Jack.

The other two looked at each other. This one's as thick as a board, they were thinking. Then, rubbing their hands, they stole away into the bushes to hide.

Jack didn't hang about on the ground. He picked the biggest tree on the edge of the clearing, climbed up it, made himself comfortable on a big bough that stretched out, and promptly went to sleep.

He was still asleep when dawn came, but

not for long. There was an ear-splitting roar, then another, and out into the space under the tree trotted the biggest, ugliest, longest-haired lion Jack had ever seen. He hadn't seen any others, but if he had, this one would have been bigger than all of them. He was enormous, he was hungry, and he sniffed the air, because he guessed his breakfast, with its clothes on, was not far away.

The lord of the forest paced around, growling and slavering, and letting off blood-curdling roars. Then suddenly, he spotted Jack, who was trying to make himself small on the branch. He began to prance up and down, reaching out with his paws and licking his lips.

All of a sudden Jack lost his balance and came down, crash. The lion was right underneath. Jack landed on the lion's back, fair and square, almost squashing the life out of the beast.

The lion raged and pranced and howled but Jack, having mounted, wasn't in a hurry to dismount. His big trouble was that he'd landed the wrong way round, but it's an ill wind that blows no good: Jack reached out in desperation and grabbed the lion's tail, just as the big brute got his breath again and tried to double back on himself to get a bite out of the big lad.

Next minute, Jack was off the lion's back, sprawled on the grass, but he still had hold of that tail. He was on his feet in a jiffy, pulling like mad, while the lion ran in circles bellowing with fury.

As the lion swung round, Jack was flung out, full length, holding on for dear life. He wheeled through the air then landed on both feet. As he did so, he pulled hard on the lion's tail and now it was milord's turn to fly through the air to land a few yards away with a crash.

Up he leapt, and Jack on the end of his tail flew forward, crash! Then the lion again – crash! – then Jack, like two of those Russian folk dancers. At each twirl they covered a dozen yards at a fine old lick.

This made such a commotion that the other two suitors jumped out of hiding, thinking the beast was masticating Jack. But when they saw the lad and lion turn and turn about, hurtling along, they took to their heels and fled back to the city, with Jack and the lion close behind.

By the time all four of them got to the city gate the news had spread and a big crowd had turned out to see the excitement, including the king and Esmerelda who came onto the palace balcony.

As the duke and the professor, neck and neck, came charging into the square, with Jack and the lion close behind, the crowd let out a great roar that sent the pigeons clattering from the roof of the palace.

Jack was so shocked by the noise that he let go of the lion's tail and the lion, released, shot forward like a thunderbolt, flattening the duke and the professor against the palace wall. Then, with a howl of rage and fright which silenced the crowd, the king of beasts took to his heels, and flew like an arrow through the square. Before him, the crowd in panic made way and the lion, still bellowing, vanished through the streets of the town, heading for open country, never to be seen again.

Back in the square, Jack slowly got to his feet. But the duke and the professor were already on the move. They fell on their knees and shouted with one voice.

"Your Majesty. We captured the lion, but that pig basher let him go again. You saw."

"You disgusting pair of cowardly cretins," shouted Esmerelda. "I saw all right."

"That'll do, my dear," said the king, who to tell truth was somewhat baffled by the speedy train of events which had just unfolded before his eyes. "The main thing is, there goes our test of heroism beyond human endurance. What do we do now?"

"I'll tell you what to do, Dad," answered Esmerelda. "Summon the three suitors to the throne room. I'll put them to the test."

"Oh?" frowned the king. "How will you do that?"

"Wait and see," said Esmerelda.

Esmerelda's Choice

Esmerelda's Choice

. . . .

While the crowd, who guessed that more excitement was to come, waited outside the palace, oohing and aahing, the three suitors, somewhat dusty and dishevelled, were conducted up the stairs into the throne room.

There, resplendent upon his royal seat, with Princess Esmerelda standing demurely beside him, sat the king. All three suitors got back their breath, bowed and waited.

"Right, my dear. Put 'em to the test."

Esmerelda rose and addressed the suitors.

"Now you must each answer me this question: how should the kingdom be ruled in future?"

Without even looking at the other two, the duke spoke first.

"Quite simply, Your Highness, with an iron hand. Stamp on your subjects and they will respect you, even if they don't like you."

"Oh dear me." Esmerelda shook her head. "You won't do. Next please."

The professor tapped his long nose and spoke very craftily. "Your Highness, you must be devious. Never tell your subjects anything. Never trust anyone and you'll never be let down."

"Oh dear me," said Esmerelda. "You won't do either. Next one please." She turned to Jack, who was gawping at her.

"You, sir, lion-catcher, how should the kingdom be governed?"

Jack didn't hesitate. He grinned and said, "Just as you like, Your Splendid Highness."

"That's the man for me," said Esmerelda.

At this there was a terrible outcry from the other two. "Majesty! You can't let a clodhopper who doesn't know his own mind rule the kingdom!" they both cried.

Esmerelda put her hands on her hips and looked them up and down.

"Very well then, what shall it be? Another

test of heroism beyond human endurance?" Turning to the king she said firmly, "Daddy, send some men to bring the lion back."

But before she had finished the sentence, the duke and the professor were already bowing their way out of the room. In two shakes of a lamb's tail they were on their way out of the palace and for all anyone knew, out of the country as well.

The king and Esmerelda led Jack onto the balcony. The king began, "May I present to you, your future king, Jack... What did you say your name was?"

But before he could answer, the crowd let out a great shout of delight. Some bright spark shouted, "Long live King Jack!" and there were more cheers.

Without further ado, they got on with the wedding, and what was even more important, they got on with the enormous wedding feast.

At the end of the evening of the feast, they found Jack fast asleep with a big happy smile on his face. Esmerelda had him carried upstairs to bed. Next day when they came down, Jack still had a smile on his face and Esmerelda had one as well.

They lived happily ever after. When the old king retired, Esmerelda and Jack ruled the kingdom. He became known as Good King John, because his mother insisted on his proper name. He was well known for his big smile, and when people came to ask for judgements or favours, Esmerelda would turn to her husband and say, "What do you think, my dear?" and Jack would say, "Just as you like, my love," and everyone was well pleased.

Smart Girls

Shortlisted for the Guardian Children's Book
Prize, these folk tales are about smart
heroines around the world.

Why is the Cow on the Roof?

Robert Leeson
Why is the Cow on the Roof?

illustrated by Axel Scheffler

Five hugely entertaining stories based on
funny folk tales from around the world.

Smart Girls
Forever

The feisty heroines of these six folk tales

all share one important quality:

they are extremely SMART!

Robert Leeson (1928–2013) wrote many books for children, including *Smart Girls* (shortlisted for the Guardian Fiction Prize), *Smart Girls Forever*, *Why is the Cow on the Roof?* and *Lucky Lad*. In 1985 he received the Eleanor Farjeon Award for his services to children's literature.

Axel Scheffler is an award-winning, internationally acclaimed illustrator of some of the most well-loved children's books, most famously *The Gruffalo*, written by Julia Donaldson. His books have been published in many languages and his work has been exhibited all around the world.